This scrapbook
belongs to:

Molly McIntire

Molly's Route 66 Adventure

ARIZONA
US
66

702 115
ILLINOIS 1946

ILLINOIS

Stuck, stuck, stuck! That's where I am. Stuck between Ricky and Brad in the back seat of a hot, stuffy car. Jill isn't coming. She's staying home for her hospital candy striping job.

"Is this trip necessary?" That's what all the wartime posters asked when roads needed to be kept clear for troop movements. It's also a very good question to ask when you're squished between two brothers in the backseat!

Dad says "We'll see the USA the American way— along Route 66!" He promises we'll see real cowboys and Indians. And *maybe* Hollywood movie stars.

Right now, all I see are Ricky's comic books. They're all over *my* part of the seat.

I can't wait to enter! Hollywood and Judy Garland, here I come!

Jill took this farewell picture of us.

I got a FREE Illinois decal and a Route 66 map just for stopping at a Royal Oil filling station. The war is over and so is gas rationing!

All the filling stations are giving away free stuff to get people to buy gas. Ricky's collecting model cars. I'm going to collect Royal Oil clues and decode them to win a signed photo of Judy Garland — DOROTHY!

Here's how my decoder works. The secret key is R6. I turn the dial so R lines up with 6, so every letter has its own secret number. The numbers 23-22-2-2-10 spell my name!

WILL ROGERS HIGHWAY   THE GRAND CANYON ROUTE
1300 MILES OF 4-LANE HIGHWAY

DRIVE US 66   **DRIVE US 66**

MAIN STREET OF AMERICA

Shortest, Fastest Year-round Best Across the Scenic West

CHICAGO to LOS ANGELES

Royal Oil

HOLLYWOOD MYSTERY CODE CONTEST

DECODER

Get a new clue every time you stop for gas!

The secret key is R6.
Now I need some clues!

ILLINOIS

FT. SHERIDAN
CHICAGO
BLACKHAWK STATE PARK
URBANA
NEW SALEM STATE PARK
SPRINGFIELD (LINCOLN TOMB)
COAL FIELDS

THE HOME OF LINCOLN

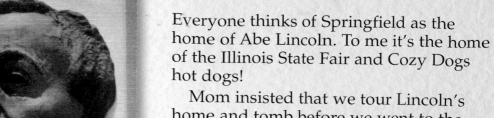

Head of Lincoln at Entrance to Tomb. Gutzon Borglum, Sculptor.

Rub here!

ORIGINAL IN HALL OF FAME WASHINGTON D.C.

ILLINOIS

mustard. Oops!

Everyone thinks of Springfield as the home of Abe Lincoln. To me it's the home of the Illinois State Fair and Cozy Dogs hot dogs!

Mom insisted that we tour Lincoln's home and tomb before we went to the fair. There's a big statue of Lincoln's head at his tomb. The nose is all shiny because people rub it for good luck.

I rubbed it hard so I will win the Royal Oil Hollywood Mystery Code Contest!

I thought Lincoln lived in a log cabin! Mom said that was before he became a lawyer.

Abraham Lincoln's Home, Springfield, Illinois

Mom was right. If we had gone to the fair first, we *never* would have left. I rode practically every ride. Brad got sick on the Spitfire.

We had cotton candy (HOORAY for no more sugar rationing!) and Cozy Dogs. A Cozy Dog is a hotdog on a stick fried in batter. I ate three!

COASTER
One Ride **25¢**
ILLINOIS STATE FAIR
061447
061447

OCTOPUS
One Ride **40¢**
ILLINOIS STATE FAIR
012747
012747

The fair was magical at night!

I warned Brad not to go on this ride!

MISSOURI AND MERAMEC CAVERNS

We crossed the mighty Mississippi River on the Chain of Rocks Bridge. Halfway across the river, the bridge curves sideways!

The barns along Route 66 are all painted with giant signs that say "Meramec Caverns." I couldn't wait to get there—out of the hot car and into the cool cave.

This was the seventh barn I saw advertising the Meramec Caverns!

MERAMEC CAVERNS
U.S. 66 MO.

CHAIN OF ROCKS BRIDGE

My first Royal Oil clue! Look out, Hollywood! Here I come!

They say Jesse James' loot is still buried here! Mom wouldn't let me stay to look for it.

© L.L.COOK CO. MILWAUKEE, WIS.   US. HY. 66   B-394
GRAPES IN WINE ROOM 4TH FLOOR — MERAMEC CAVERNS, STANTON, MO.

In the cave, a guide led us along underground passages lit by thousands of tiny lights. The echoes and the spooky shadows sent shivers down my spine. Especially when I heard that Jesse James and his gang had used the place as a hideout!

The guide said people have underground dances and even weddings in the cavern's Grand Ballroom. That's SO romantic!

CHILDREN: 25¢ ADULTS: $1
MERAMEC CAVERNS
Stanton, Missouri
007025 007025

Royal Oil

ROYAL OIL HOLLYWOOD
MYSTERY CODE CONTEST

Use your Royal Oil Decoder!
(The secret key is R6.)

First Clue: 13-16-19-6-19

MERAMEC CAVERNS
STANTON MO.
JESSE JAMES' HIDEOUT!
ON HIGHWAY 66

MISSOURI

THAT RAT RICKY! Our first time camping as a family ever, and Ricky practically spoiled the whole thing!

We had a perfect campsite — right next to Little Piney Creek. We cooked beans in Dad's old Army mess kit. We even had s'mores and baked apples, just like at Camp Gowonagin!

This is our brand-new tent.

I found these tracks on our hike — just like Sacagawea!

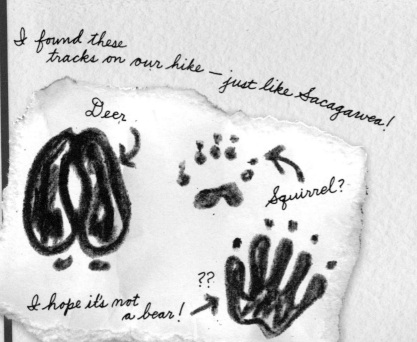

Deer

Squirrel?

I hope it's not a bear! *??*

MY CAMPFIRE BAKED APPLES

1. Remove cores of Granny Smith apples.

2. Fill centers with brown sugar, cinnamon, and raisins.

3. Wrap in foil. Bury in warm, ash-covered coals for 20 minutes (until soft).

4. Serve with spoons.

My recipe was a big hit!

I couldn't wait to crawl inside our brand-new tent and snuggle into my sleeping bag. I felt IT the minute I stuck my foot into my bag—something long and slimy and squiggly! Eeeeuuuwww!

I tore out of that tent like lightning and ran smack into Ricky. Right away I knew it was a trick. Ricky bought that rubber snake at the Mule Trading Post, just to ruin my first camping trip! I'll get that rat Ricky back somehow, if it's the last thing I do!

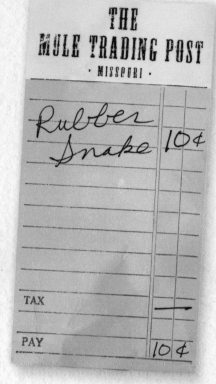

THE
MULE TRADING POST
· MISSOURI ·

Rubber Snake 10¢

TAX

PAY 10¢

MISSOURI

ST. JOSEPH
JEFFERSON CITY
KANSAS CITY
INDEPENDENCE
VERSAILLES
ST. LOUIS
CAMDENTON
SPRINGFIELD

Ricky says he doesn't know anything about any snake, but I've got proof!

I got this at the Ranger Station. Arithmetic even on vacation?!

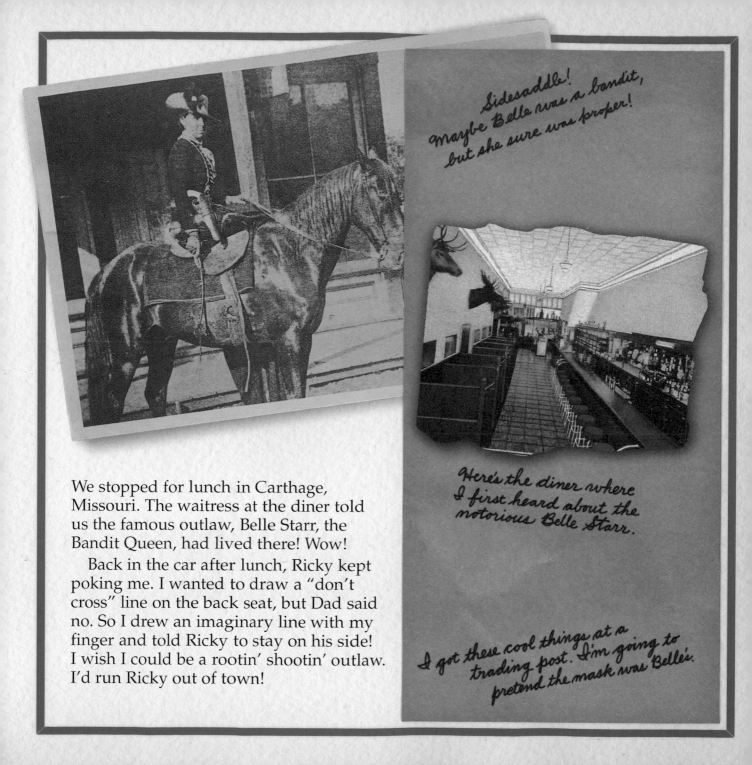

Sidesaddle! Maybe Belle was a bandit, but she sure was proper!

Here's the diner where I first heard about the notorious Belle Starr.

We stopped for lunch in Carthage, Missouri. The waitress at the diner told us the famous outlaw, Belle Starr, the Bandit Queen, had lived there! Wow!

Back in the car after lunch, Ricky kept poking me. I wanted to draw a "don't cross" line on the back seat, but Dad said no. So I drew an imaginary line with my finger and told Ricky to stay on his side! I wish I could be a rootin' shootin' outlaw. I'd run Ricky out of town!

I got these cool things at a trading post. I'm going to pretend the mask was Belle's.

We were only in Kansas for 13 miles, but I still got a sticker!

KANSAS
Waving Fields of Grain
LEAVENWORTH
TOPEKA
FT. RILEY   KANSAS CITY
SCOTT CTY. STATE PARK   PAWNEE ROCK   FT. SCOTT
DODGE CITY   WICHITA
115

KANSAS

We almost got hit by a tornado! We were listening to the radio and, all of a sudden, an air raid siren sounded — with no war on. It was a tornado!

The sky turned an icky green. The air got really still. Then it started to rain and blow so hard Dad had to pull over!

We all got down on the floor of the car and waited until the rain stopped. We never did see the tornado, but I'm sure it was really close — just like in the *Wizard of Oz!*

A tornado that can do this could take Dorothy over a rainbow!

We made it through the tornado OK!

OKLAHOMA

CHEROKEE   TULSA   WILL ROGERS MEM.

OKLAHOMA CITY

FORT SILL   KIAMICHI MTS.

Everything's goin' OKAY

OKLAHOMA!

I've started singing "O-o-o-o-klahoma!" It's driving Ricky nuts!

We kids were all excited about crossing the Oklahoma line. Sometimes people see a ball of fire there called a "spooklight" that bounces around the sky. It wasn't dark enough, or I'm sure we'd have seen it!

We got to stop at Galloway's Totem Pole Park. They're building the world's tallest totem pole there. When it's done, it will be over 90 feet tall. That's 15 times taller than Dad. Ricky thought it was cool. But I know that Southwest Indians didn't build totem poles. And they *certainly* didn't build them out of cement!

This is what the giant totem pole will look like.

I think real totem poles are better.

Jeepers. Oklahoma must go on *forever!* We've been driving for hours and still no cowboys or Indians. That is, unless you count Will Rogers. He was a cowboy *and* an Indian (part Cherokee).

We learned all about him at the Will Rogers Memorial. We saw his rodeo trophies, saddles, and movie costumes. He did everything! He was a trick roper, a radio celebrity, a film star, an author, and a newspaper writer.

He named his trick horse "Teddy" after his best friend, President Theodore (Teddy) Roosevelt.

Will Rogers (and Teddy)

In Afton, the Route 66 sign is painted right on the road! The road is so narrow it almost looks like a sidewalk.

The dirt is RED here!

OKLAHOMA

Near Tulsa, Mom and Dad had a surprise for us—a movie! They gave us a choice. We could see *The Yearling* at a regular theater. Or, we could see *National Velvet* at an outdoor drive-in theater. Even Ricky wanted to go to the drive-in!

When it got dark, we snuggled under Dad's old army blankets to watch the show.

In the winter, people have to use car heaters.

Selected POP CORN

MAJORETTE

BIG SCREEN
DRIVE-IN THEATRE
ROUTE 66 — *"Just Outside of Tulsa"*

HOW TO USE YOUR HEATER...

FIND SPEAKER POST WITH A RED LIGHT THIS IS A HEATER POST

1. PLACE YOUR HEATER ON FLOOR OF AUTO, RUN CORD THRU WINDOW TO SPEAKER POST!

2. INSERT PLUG INTO RECEPTACLE ON SPEAKER POST

3. SWITCH TOP OF HEATER FOR ON AND OFF!

4. IN EVENT OF DIFFICULTY WITH UNIT, REPLACEMENTS ARE AVAILABLE AT REFRESHMENT STAND.

When Leaving — Disconnect Heater — Wrap Cord Around Heater — Use Exit Only And Surrender Heater To Attendant At Exit or Brass Check If No Heater Was Obtained!

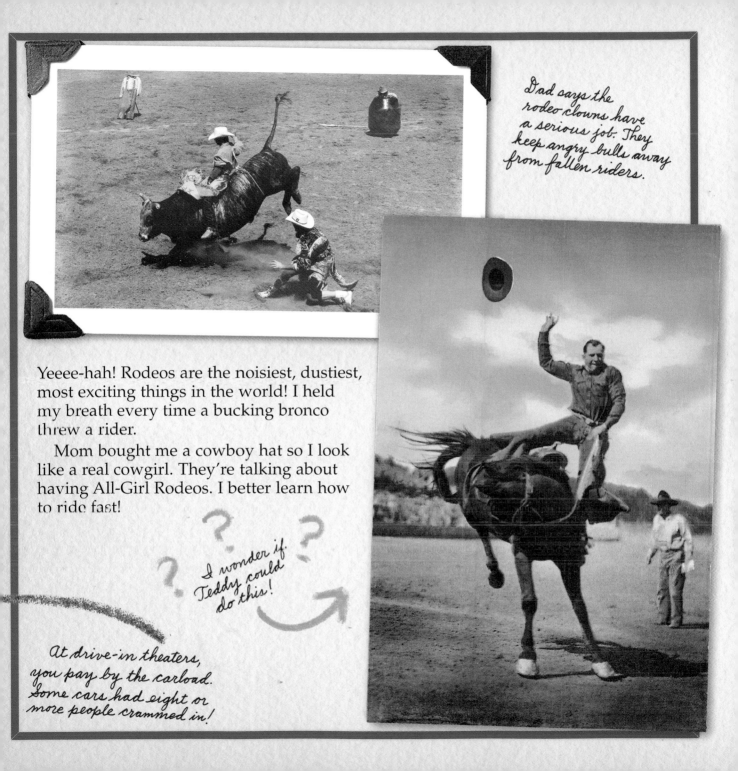

Dad says the rodeo clowns have a serious job. They keep angry bulls away from fallen riders.

Yeeee-hah! Rodeos are the noisiest, dustiest, most exciting things in the world! I held my breath every time a bucking bronco threw a rider.

Mom bought me a cowboy hat so I look like a real cowgirl. They're talking about having All-Girl Rodeos. I better learn how to ride fast!

I wonder if Teddy could do this!

At drive-in theaters, you pay by the carload. Some cars had eight or more people crammed in!

TEXAS

This is the Texas "panhandle."
It doesn't look like a pan
handle to me!

Everything in Texas is BIG and LOOONG. Especially the road. It goes on forever!

People call this part of Texas the "High Plains." I call it the "Empty Plains" because there is nothing to see. I bought a desert animals postcard so I could look for animals. But I think they're as hot as I am and they're all hiding.

We saw a sign for the Regal Reptile Ranch. Dad wouldn't stop. Rats. I wanted to get Ricky a pet rattlesnake!

I've got half my clues.
Will we ever get to Hollywood?

ROYAL OIL HOLLYWOOD
MYSTERY CODE CONTEST

Use your Royal Oil Decoder!
(The secret key is R6.)

Royal Oil

Third Clue: 18-22

It's so hot, the rattlers are shedding their skins! Ha ha!

I'm SO hot! (Did I say that already?) It must be 500° in this car! Every time I move, my legs stick to the seat. Mom keeps suggesting car games, but it's too hot to even think.

The only game that's fun is the Burma-Shave game. Burma-Shave sells shaving cream. They put rhyming signs all along the road. The first person to see a sign (usually me!) gets to read all the signs in the rhyme out loud.

This is my favorite:

PAST SCHOOLHOUSES

TAKE IT SLOW

LET THE LITTLE

SHAVERS GROW

BURMA-SHAVE

700 MILES DESERT
WATER BAGS
THERMOS JUGS ICE

I got scared when I saw this. But Dad said we had plenty of water.

TEXAS

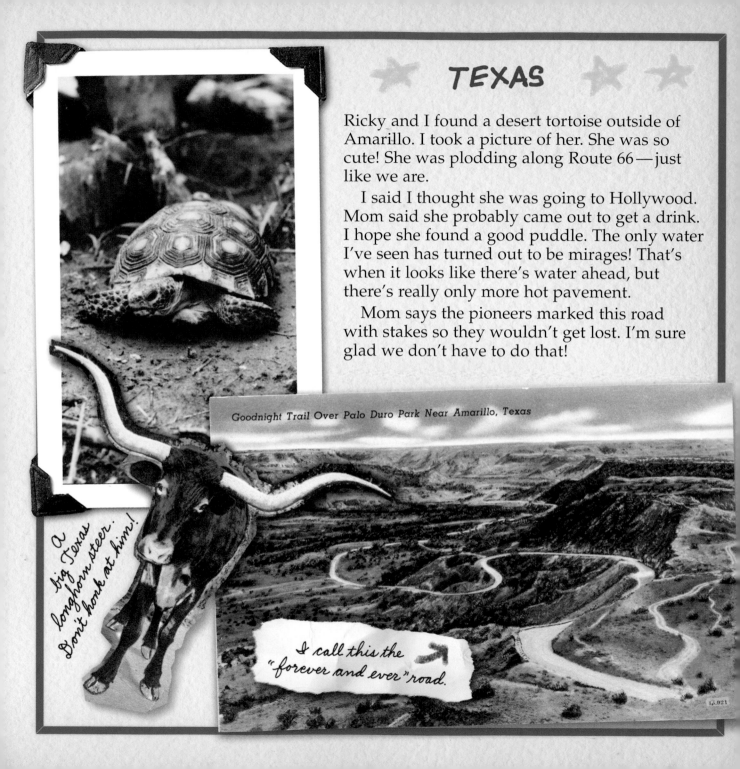

Ricky and I found a desert tortoise outside of Amarillo. I took a picture of her. She was so cute! She was plodding along Route 66—just like we are.

I said I thought she was going to Hollywood. Mom said she probably came out to get a drink. I hope she found a good puddle. The only water I've seen has turned out to be mirages! That's when it looks like there's water ahead, but there's really only more hot pavement.

Mom says the pioneers marked this road with stakes so they wouldn't get lost. I'm sure glad we don't have to do that!

Goodnight Trail Over Palo Duro Park Near Amarillo, Texas

A big Texas longhorn steer. Don't honk at him!

I call this the "forever and ever" road.

Just when I thought we were totally lost in the Texas desert, the Road Runner Restaurant popped up. Boy, was I glad!

In the restaurant window, there was a poster asking women to give their factory jobs back to men, now that the men are done being soldiers. It's not fair! Women are good welders and riveters, too! Why can't they just make more jobs?

Road Runner
RESTAURANT AND SODA GRILL

TABLE NO.	NO. PERSONS	CHECK NO.	SERVER NO.
9	5	16884	1

1 Chick Sal on Roll	45
1 Swiss Cheese	30
3 Peanut Butter	75
2 Iced Tea	30
3 Jello	45
3 Dbl I.C. Soda (Choc/Van/Straw)	75

Thanks!
PLEASE PAY CASHIER $3.00

NATIONAL CHECKING CO., CHICAGO, NEW YORK, ST. PAUL, KANSAS CITY.

There's TONGUE on this menu! Eeeeeyuck!

DESSERTS

SOUTHERN PECAN PIE 20¢
Pound Cake 15¢
Coffee Cake (Heated if Desired) 15¢
Rice Pudding, Cream 15¢
Orange Sherbet 15¢
Apple Pie (Hot or Cold) 15¢
Strawberry, Vanilla
 or Chocolate Ice Cream 20¢

Fresh Strawberries and Cream 35¢
Chocolate Pudding 15¢
Cocoanut Layer Cake 15¢
Jell-O 15¢
Assorted French Pastry 15¢
Chilled Watermelon 20¢
Fresh Peaches with Cream 25¢

MARBLE LAYER CAKE 15¢
Chocolate or Mocha Layer Cake 15¢
Cup Custard 15¢
Peach Pie 15¢

Soda Fountain

MALTED MILK
Choice of Flavors, Ice Cream
25¢

MILK SHAKE
Choice of Flavors
25¢

DOUBLE ICE CREAM SODA
Choice of Flavors
25¢

SPECIAL SUNDAE
35¢
(Vanilla and Chocolate Ice Cream, Topped with Marshmallow, Chopped Pecans, Whipped Cream and Cherry)

NEW MEXICO

Two more clues to go!

Hola from New Mexico! It feels more like *Old* Mexico to me. In some towns, more people speak Spanish than English.

Ha! I finally got Ricky back! Dad found the greatest desert swimming hole. It's called the "Blue Hole" because it's so blue and deep. We changed into our suits behind some yucca plants. Ricky was so busy showing off, he left his clothes behind. Guess what was gone when he went back to look!

Ricky— GOTCHA!

NEW MEXICO

AZTEC   SANTA FE
• GALLUP
  • ALBUQUERQUE
FT. SUMNER
WHITE
SANDS   CARLSBAD
LAS
CRUCES   CAVERNS

— The Spanish State —

L-130

New Mexico feels like a whole different country!

CACTUS

MOTOR   LODGE

TUCUMCARI • NEW MEXICO

We stayed here. Tucumcari is named after two Indian sweethearts — Tocom and Kari.

CACTUS
MOTOR
LODGE
NEW MEXICO'S FINEST
STEAM HEATED

East on U. S. Highway 66 at City Limit

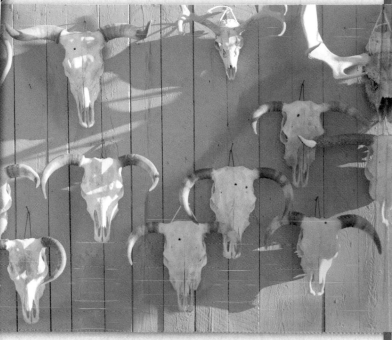

This dance is called "El Jarabe Tapátio"
(el ha-RA-beh tah-PAH-tee-oh). It's also
called the Mexican Hat Dance.

We passed through a tiny town that was having a
fiesta. There was singing and dancing everywhere!

Dad bought me a beautiful heart-shaped charm
called a *milagro* (mee-LAH-gro). Milagro means
"miracle" in Spanish. He said my milagro will
remind me of my love for my friends, family, and
the whole world. And it's a reminder that miracles
happen every day.

We're half way to Santa Monica. Only 1,119 miles
to go! That's *today's* miracle!

My milagro.

NEW MEXICO

The Acoma Pueblo is a real Indian village. The Indians don't look anything like they do in the movies! People have lived here for almost 1,000 years. Their homes are carved out of rock on top of a mesa. (That's a flat-topped mountain.) We had to climb a million stone steps to get up there. No wonder it's called the "Sky City"!

I climbed up here!

Mom was strict with us at the pueblo. She said, "No running around. This is their home!"

"Sky City"

Acoma Pueblo

**CLINES CORNERS
CURIO SHOP**

P. O. Encino, New Mexico

Sun Symbol =
Happiness

NEW MEXICO

Horse = Journey

Crossed
Arrows =
Friendship

We got to the town of Gallup just in time for a giant festival called the Inter-tribal Indian Ceremonial. Thousands of people from different tribes come here every year for dances, craft shows, and even a rodeo.

I made friends with a Navajo girl. She was dressed just like the girl in my Clines Corners brochure! When I told her I wished *I* could dress like that every day, she laughed! She said she was just dressed up for the festival. On regular days, she dresses like I do. Jeepers, did I feel dumb.

ARIZONA

The Painted Desert looks as if someone took a giant paintbrush and brushed red, purple, and blue strokes all over the rocks. Really!

In the Petrified Forest, we climbed on giant stone logs. Dad said 150 million years ago, the logs were buried in the sand. Water seeped into them and filled them with minerals. That's why they're rock hard and filled with beautiful crystals. I felt like I was in a forest of jewels!

PAINTED DESERT

I wish my pictures could show the purple crystals inside these logs!

METEOR CRATER, ARIZONA

I'd call Arizona "The Land of Big Surprises."

My fifth clue. Maybe Judy Garland will be in Hollywood to give me my prize!

At first I didn't believe a giant meteor could ever hit Earth. Well, now I do! What else could have made a mile-wide hole right in the middle of a desert?

We climbed up the observatory tower to get a good look at the crater. Some of the boulders along the rim are as big as our house. I still wonder, though: Whatever happened to the meteor?

THANK YOU!

Cottage No. 1   Paid $ 1.50

Trailer Space _____   Paid $ _____

CACTUS GARDENS COURT
MR. and MRS. J. H. GATES
Gas, Oil, Curios
HIGHWAY 66   2 MILES EAST OF FLAGSTAFF, ARIZ.

Ricky sat on a cactus here and got his backside full of spines!

ARIZONA ～ AND THE

We took a side trip off Route 66 to see the Grand Canyon. GRAND doesn't come close to describing it! How about HUMONGOUS Canyon?

From the North rim, it looks like a giant paint pot, which is what some people call it. We're staying at the Bright Angel Lodge. Mom and Dad said we can take a mule ride into the canyon tomorrow. But we have to *promise* to be careful. In some places, the canyon is one mile deep!

President Teddy Roosevelt said every American should see the Grand Canyon.

H-4472   THE LOBBY, BRIGHT ANGEL LODGE, GRAND CANYON NATIONAL PARK, ARIZONA

GRAND CANYON!!

We almost lost Ricky! It happened on our mule ride. Of course, Ricky was goofing off. Then, suddenly, he wasn't on his mule anymore! I was *sure* he'd fallen to the bottom of the Canyon!

It turns out he just slipped down a little drop-off. Boy, were we relieved when the mule guide pulled him back up! I might want to get rid of Ricky sometimes, but not for good!

I'm glad I didn't see the Ranger jump!

I made a rubbing of a clam fossil. 250 million years ago, this canyon was under water!

NEVADA ~ BOULDER DAM ~

I thought California was our last state. But Dad wanted to take a "quick" side trip off Route 66 to *Nevada* to see the Boulder Dam. Mom said the dam is only 93 miles from California—and my *last* clue!—so I guess I can wait.

Dad was nervous about driving on top of the dam. On the Lake Mead side, the water's 500 feet deep!

My last clue!
I've cracked the code!

ROYAL OIL HOLLYWOOD MYSTERY CODE CONTEST

Use your Royal Oil Decoder!
(The secret key is R6.)

Royal Oil

Sixth Clue: 16 - 22 - 23 - 19

We heard the water rush under our car!

1B-H2433

CALIFORN...

Summertime...all the time

DEATH VALLEY
LOS ANGELES
SAN JUAN
CAPISTRANO

SANTA MONICA, CALIFORNIA

The Pacific Ocean!

CALIFORNIA

California! At last! We drove for miles across the hot, hot sand of the Mojave Desert. When we reached Santa Monica, we headed straight for the Santa Monica Pier on the Pacific Ocean. As soon as Dad stopped the car, I jumped out and ran to touch the water. I tasted it, too, to make sure it was salty.

There was a giant carousel on the Santa Monica pier. I rode it twice!

This was my horse!

We hung a water bag on our car's hood. As long as we kept moving, the water kept our engine cool.

MOJAVE WATER BAG

Judy Garland's hand and foot prints.

FOR MR. GRAUMAN
ALL HAPPINESS
Judy "Garland

I had fun at the Pier, but I wanted to get to Hollywood right away to get my prize. But first, Mom wanted to stop at the "Forecourt" at the Grauman's Chinese Theatre. She wanted to see the stars' footprints. By the time I got to the Royal Oil station, I was SO nervous! What if I got all the clues wrong?

But I was right! The secret message was "THERE IS NO PLACE LIKE HOME." That's what Judy Garland, I mean Dorothy, says to Auntie Em!

And there's no place like some of the other places I've seen on Route 66, either!

A WORLD PREMIERE NIGHT IN HOLLYWOOD

Hollywood is SO beautiful!

Sincerely,
Judy Garland

MY PRIZE!

Well, I didn't get to meet Judy Garland. But guess what? I got LOTS of kicks on Route 66!

Published by Pleasant Company Publications
Copyright © 2002 by Pleasant Company
Produced by becker&mayer!, Bellevue, WA
www.beckermayer.com

Printed and assembled in China
02 03 04 05 C&C 10 9 8 7 6 5 4 3 2 1
The American Girls Collection®, Molly®, Molly McIntire®, and the American Girl logo are trademarks of Pleasant Company.

Visit Pleasant Company's Web site at: americangirl.com

Written by Dottie Raymer
Edited by Jodi Evert and Carol P. Garzona
Art Directed by Will Capellaro and Jane S. Varda
Designed by Amy Redmond
Cover and page 2 illustration of McIntire family by Nick Backes
All other interior illustration by Amy Redmond
Calligraphy by Linda P. Hancock
Researched by Kathy Borkowski, Sally Wood, Dottie Raymer, and
    Carol P. Garzona
Photography by Keith Megay
Production coordinated by Mary Cudnofsky and Barbara Galvani

Special thanks to David Knudson, National Historic Route 66 Federation; Michael Wallis, author of *Route 66: The Mother Road*; Shellee Graham, author of *Tales from the Coral Court: Photos and Stories from a Lost Route 66 Landmark;* Joan S. Raymer; Judy Garland Museum; and Angel Alvarado.

IMAGE CREDITS

Every effort has been made to correctly attribute all the material reproduced in this book. If any errors have unknowingly occurred, we will be happy to correct them in future editions.

State decals: from *Route 66: The Mother Road* (St. Martin's Press) by Michael Wallis; ILLINOIS — Pump, adapted from image in Rancho Cucamonga Visitors Center collection; Map adapted from image by National U.S. 66 Highway Assn.; Lincoln Tomb, Lincoln Souvenir & Gift Shop; Lincoln Home, H. N. Shonkwiler; Fair photos, *Popular Science*, July 1949; MISSOURI — Barn, Terrence Moore; Bridge, MWM Co.; Meramec postcards, L.L. Cook Co.; Tent, Montgomery Ward catalog, Spring-Summer 1941; *Ranger 'Rithmetic*, adapted from U.S. Department of Agriculture, Forest Service book; Belle Starr postcard, unknown; Poster, unknown; Diner, Wallis Collection; KANSAS — Tornado, unknown; OKLAHOMA — Totem Pole, Roger's County Historical Society; Will Rogers, Will Rogers Memorial; Dog, Shellee Graham collection; Drive-In, *Drive-in Movie Memories* by Don and Susan Sanders; Bull Rider in Rodeo Iowa, USA, Corbis; Bronco Rider, Doubleday & Co.; TEXAS — Animals postcard, Western Resort Publications & Novelty; Desert, Terrence Moore; Tortoise, Jerry Novak; Steer and Road postcard, West Texas News Agency; Blue Hole, Richard R. Delgado; Tucumcari, Associate Service; Dancers, from *A Treasury of Mexican Folkways* by Frances Toor; Skulls, Shellee Graham collection; NEW MEXICO — Acoma Pueblo, Detroit Publishing Co.; Sky City, Petley Studios; Navajo, Bradshaw's Color Studios; Clines Corners brochure, unknown; ARIZONA — Painted Desert, unknown; Petrified Logs, Petley Studios; Meteor Crater, Petley Studios; Grand Canyon, Herz Post Cards; Lodge, unknown; GRAND CANYON — Mule Ride, Santa Fe RR Collection, Grand Canyon National Park #67374, circa 1947–8; Ranger, Southwest Post Card Co.; NEVADA — Dam, Desert Souvenir Supply; CALIFORNIA — Santa Monica, Western Publishing & Novelty Co.; Carousel, Santa Monica Public Library Archives; HOLLYWOOD — Forecourt, Jim and Maurine Wilke, permission from the Mann's Chinese Theatre; Hollywood postcard, Western Publishing & Novelty Co.; Judy Garland "fan photo," Peter Cobbin collection. CREDIT PAGE — decal, unknown.

HAVE A SAFE TRIP
Come back soon!

MORE TO DISCOVER!

While books are the heart of The American Girls Collection,®
they are only the beginning. The stories in the Collection
come to life when you act them out with the beautiful
American Girls dolls and their exquisite clothes and accessories.

To request a free catalogue full of things girls love, send in this
postcard, call **1-800-845-0005,** or visit our Web site at **americangirl.com**.

Please send me an American Girl® catalogue.

My name is _____

My address is _____

City _____ State _____ Zip _____

1961i

My birth date is _____/_____/_____ E-mail address _____
month day year

Parent's signature _____

And send a catalogue to my friend.

My friend's name is _____

Address _____

City _____ State _____ Zip _____

1225i

If the postcard has already been removed from this book
and you would like to receive an American Girl® catalogue,
please send your name and address to:

American Girl
P.O. Box 620497
Middleton, WI 53562-0497

You may also call our toll-free number, **1-800-845-0005**,
or visit our Web site at **americangirl.com**.

PO BOX 620497
MIDDLETON WI 53562-0497

THE BOOKS ABOUT MOLLY

MEET MOLLY • An American Girl
While her father is fighting in World War Two,
Molly and her brother start their own war at home.

MOLLY LEARNS A LESSON • A School Story
Molly and her friends plan a secret project to help the
war effort, and learn about allies and cooperation.

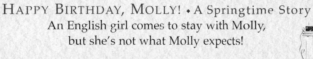

MOLLY'S SURPRISE • A Christmas Story
Molly makes plans for Christmas surprises,
but she ends up being surprised herself.

HAPPY BIRTHDAY, MOLLY! • A Springtime Story
An English girl comes to stay with Molly,
but she's not what Molly expects!

MOLLY SAVES THE DAY • A Summer Story
At summer camp, Molly has to pretend to be her
friend's enemy and face her own fears, too.

CHANGES FOR MOLLY • A Winter Story
Dad will return from the war any day! Will he arrive in time
to see the "grown-up" Molly perform as Miss Victory?

◆

WELCOME TO MOLLY'S WORLD • 1944
American history is lavishly illustrated
with photographs, illustrations, and
excerpts from real girls' letters and diaries.